Christmas
in
Haggerty

D1272646

THE HAGGERTY MYSTERY NOVELS
BY BETSY BRANNON GREEN:

Hearts in Hiding

Until Proven Guilty

Above Suspicion

Silenced

Copycat

Poison

Double Cross

OTHER NOVELS
BY BETSY BRANNON GREEN:

Never Look Back

Don't Close Your Eyes

Foul Play

Christmas in Haggerty

✳ *A Novel* ✳

BETSY BRANNON GREEN

Covenant Communications, Inc.

Published by Covenant Communications, Inc.
American Fork, Utah

Printed in Canada
First Printing: October 2006

12 11 10 09 08 07 06   10 9 8 7 6 5 4 3 2

ISBN 1-59156-896-X

*This book is dedicated to
all the family history center workers across the world
who invest countless hours in their efforts
to make families forever.*

CHAPTER ONE

Eugenia Atkins stared up at a cobweb on her bedroom ceiling and tried to ignore her dog, Lady, who was barking ferociously. It was past time for their regular morning walk, but somewhere during the night Eugenia had come to the conclusion that her neighbors, the Iversons, were never coming home. After hours of dwelling on this dismal prospect, she was now too depressed to get up, even for a refreshing walk with her little dog.

Eugenia had lived all of her seventy-seven years in the small town of Haggerty, Georgia. She and her husband, Charles, had never been blessed with children, and when he died suddenly, her life seemed meaningless. Then Kate and Mark Iverson had moved into the old Riley house next door. Their first child, Emily, was born almost immediately, and their son, Charles, followed a year later. Since the Iversons' arrival, Eugenia had been busy and happy, helping them raise their family.

But the Iversons left for an extended visit with relatives at the end of October. Mark was the resident agent for the FBI in nearby Albany. He spoke Spanish fluently, and with degrees in accounting and law, he was well qualified for a high-paying job in the corporate world. Eugenia lived in fear that some company would make him an offer he couldn't refuse. She had barely survived Thanksgiving without them, and now Christmas was approaching with no sign of their return. Indulging in a rare moment of self-pity, Eugenia burrowed deeper under her old comforter.

Lady continued to bark pitifully, and Eugenia's resolve weakened a few minutes later when the phone rang. It was her sister, Annabelle, who said, "Derrick has been assigned to bring eggnog to the library's Christmas party tonight so I need my antique crystal punchbowl back."

Since Eugenia was in a bad mood already, this ridiculous statement annoyed her more than usual. "Why are you telling me?" she asked. "I don't have your punchbowl."

"Yes, you do," Annabelle insisted. "You borrowed it last month for Thanksgiving dinner at the retirement home."

"I *asked* you if I could borrow it," Eugenia conceded. "But you said it was too fragile and too valuable to use around all those clumsy old people."

"I said no such thing!" Annabelle denied. "You were the only clumsy old person I would have worried about!"

"In any case," Eugenia said. "I didn't use your punchbowl. I borrowed Polly's instead."

"You've always been jealous that Mother left the punchbowl to me," Annabelle continued senselessly.

"Annabelle," Eugenia began, intending to tell her sister that she was too depressed to fight about an old punchbowl, but Annabelle interrupted her.

"It's missing, and I know you have it!"

"The very idea!" Eugenia lost patience and hung up the phone. She wasn't above *borrowing* something from Annabelle, but in this case she was completely innocent. Closing her eyes, Eugenia tried to drift back to sleep. Then she heard someone knocking on her front door.

Frowning, Eugenia squinted at the alarm clock on her bedside table. It was seven o'clock in the morning. According to her mother's version of Southern etiquette, the only acceptable reason to knock on someone's door that early was a death in the immediate family. Eugenia knew that if one of her few remaining cousins had died, Annabelle would have mentioned that before making accusations of petty punchbowl theft.

Eugenia considered her options. She could ignore the knocking and hope that whoever it was would go away, but then she'd be left with the question of who and why. Knowing curiosity would drive her crazy, Eugenia picked up the phone and called her neighbor Polly Kirby.

Since the angle was wrong, Polly couldn't see Eugenia's front porch. But there was a chance that the nosy neighbor had seen someone walk up the sidewalk. Polly finally answered on the fourth ring—an absolute dereliction of her normal busy-body duties. "Hello?"

Eugenia propped herself up on an elbow and asked, "What took you so long to answer?"

"I was in the bathtub," Polly replied.

Unfortunately, the only time Polly wasn't answering her phone *or* looking out one of her many windows was when she was in the bathtub. "So I guess you didn't see who walked up my front sidewalk and is now knocking on my door?"

"Someone's knocking on your door at seven o'clock in the morning?" Polly cried. "Did one of your relatives die overnight?"

"Not that I know of."

"Oh, that's good." Polly sounded relieved. "So why don't you just open the door and see who it is?"

Eugenia decided that this was a good opportunity to prepare Polly and the rest of the community for the fact that she was going into a decline. "I can't open the door because I'm not dressed," she said. "In fact, I'm still in bed."

She heard her neighbor gasp. "Usually you've been up for hours by now! I hope you don't have the flu."

No, Eugenia thought to herself. *Now that Kate and Mark have taken the children away, I just don't have any reason to live.* To Polly she said, "I don't have the flu." The knocking began again, more insistent this time. Eugenia sighed and pushed back the comforter. "Obviously my visitor isn't going away, so I guess I'll have to get up."

"I hope you feel better soon," Polly told her.

"Thanks," Eugenia muttered as she disconnected the call. She pulled on a pink terrycloth bathrobe that had seen better days and stuck her feet into a pair of ragged chenille slippers. Then she headed downstairs with Lady nipping at her heels.

When Eugenia reached the entryway, she squinted against the early morning sunlight streaming cheerfully through the windows in complete disregard for her depressed condition. Making a mental note to purchase some thick shades soon, she pulled open the door and blinked twice to be sure her old eyes weren't playing tricks on her.

The entire Iverson family was standing on the porch, and in that instant the loneliness of the past few weeks seemed to disappear, and all was right with Eugenia's world. Forgetting her dignity, she threw her arms around Kate—who just happened to be the closest.

"I declare, I don't know when I've been so glad to see anybody!" Eugenia cried as Lady rushed out, barking ecstatically at their guests.

"Surprise!" Emily and little Charles chorused.

"You all should know better than to surprise an old woman," Eugenia scolded half-heartedly as she released Kate and drew the children into a hug. "Are you trying to give me a stroke?"

Emily frowned. "We thought you'd be happy to see us."

"We thought you'd be happy," Charles concurred.

"I am," Eugenia assured them. "Just give me a minute to catch my breath."

"Do you have tea cakes?" Charles asked.

"No, but I can make some," Eugenia replied. "And the two of you can help me."

Emily turned to her mother for permission. "Is that okay, Mama?"

"Please," Charles begged.

Kate nodded. "It will be easier to get the van unpacked without the two of you underfoot."

Eugenia held the front door open wide. "Take Lady inside, and wait for me in the kitchen." Once the children were gone, she addressed Mark. "So have you come back to Haggerty to pack up your furniture?"

Mark and Kate regarded her with equally blank looks. Finally Mark said, "Pack our furniture?"

"Aren't you moving?" Eugenia demanded bravely.

Mark shook his head. "No, we're not moving."

"Georgia is our home," Kate added.

Tears prickled Eugenia's eyes. "Well you've been away from *home* for a mighty long time."

"We've been ready to come back for weeks, but the FBI just gave Mark permission to return yesterday," Kate said. "We were so anxious to get here that we drove through the night."

Eugenia was mollified by this explanation but didn't want to appear totally desperate, so she scrutinized them. "That would explain your disheveled appearance."

Kate laughed. "I've missed your particular brand of Southern hospitality."

"Hmph!" Eugenia responded.

"We aren't moving, but we do have an announcement to make," Kate continued.

As long as they weren't moving, Eugenia figured she could handle anything else. "What kind of announcement?"

"There's been a big shake-up at the FBI offices in Atlanta," Kate provided. "The Special-Agent-in-Charge was given early retirement, and several of his key people were transferred, including Mark's supervisor, Dan Davis."

"Because of that business in Colombia?" Eugenia guessed, and Mark nodded.

Kate beamed up at her husband. "They offered Mark the supervisor job in Atlanta!"

Eugenia clutched her heart. "Atlanta," she whispered.

Mark didn't seem to notice her distress. "But I don't want to relocate."

"So the FBI is going to let him supervise from Albany," Kate finished for him. "They're expanding his office and hiring some new people for him to boss around."

Mark rolled his eyes, but Eugenia ignored Kate's joke. "So you'll still work in Albany?" she confirmed.

Mark nodded. "And we'll still live right here in Haggerty."

Kate addressed Eugenia. "What do you have to say about *that*?"

Anxious to hide her slip into sentimentality, Eugenia pointed toward the Iversons' house. "If you're here to stay, you'd better hurry and get some Christmas decorations up. The Haggerty Beautification Committee has challenged everyone to decorate their front doors, and you're the only folks on Maple Street who aren't participating."

"A door decoration contest?" Kate murmured. "That's a first."

"It's intended to encourage community pride and emphasize the real meaning of Christmas,"

Eugenia informed her. "The theme is 'What Christmas Means to Me,' and the doors will be judged on Christmas Eve. Prizes will be awarded in several different categories."

Kate gave her front door a speculative glance. "I wonder what we'll get if we win."

Mark took his wife by the elbow and propelled her toward their van. "Before we worry about winning the door-decorating contest, we need to get unpacked."

Eugenia was too happy to have them home to comment on Mark's lack of Christmas spirit.

"You two go ahead," she called after them. "By the time you're done, the children and I should have some fresh tea cakes waiting." Then, with a smile on her face, Eugenia headed toward her kitchen.

CHAPTER TWO

Kate Iverson carefully navigated the attic ladder, balancing the box of leftover Christmas decorations on one hip. As she walked down the stairs, her free hand brushed the artificial garland twisted along the banister. When she reached the entryway, she put the box on the round table in the center of the room with a sigh.

Two weeks had passed since their return home. Every day she promised herself that she would decorate her front door and show the residents of Haggerty what Christmas meant to her. But every night for the past two weeks she'd gone to bed with that task uncompleted. Since the Iversons had been using the same decorating scheme every Christmas since the year they married, "decking" the house had required little thought and no imagination.

But this year the front door was a different matter. It was unthinkable that the Iversons' door would be the only one in town that remained unadorned. And the holly wreath covered with fake gingerbread men that they'd used in the past had nothing to do with the real meaning of Christmas.

She glanced down at the box, hoping its contents would help her. A quick inventory told her there wasn't much to work with. Just a few strands of white lights, broken ornaments, and some spray-painted pinecones. At the bottom was a plastic nativity set she had purchased when Emily was a baby. It was missing several pieces now, but she smiled as she remembered how much Emily had enjoyed playing with it. She picked up Baby Jesus, and as her fingers folded around the little manger bed, her smile faded and tears began to fall.

"Kate!" Mark called from the back door. "I was on my way to Tifton for a meeting when I realized I had left a file here . . ." He reached the entryway and saw her. "Aw, Kate. What's the matter?"

She held out her hand so he could see the plastic baby. "I don't know why I've been so blue lately. Maybe it's because all your brothers have new babies."

She raised her eyes to his. "I don't want to spoil everyone's Christmas, but I just want a baby so much."

He crossed the room and gathered her into his arms. She pressed her damp cheek against the crisp fabric of his dress shirt. "It's not that I don't accept the Lord's will," she told him. "And I'm very thankful for the two children we have . . ."

"I know."

She took a deep breath, then continued, "Charles wants a racecar bed like Mason Ragsdale's, but every time I think about putting away the crib and the rocking chair and that fake antique quilted wall hanging . . ."

"Charles can stay in the crib a while longer."

She swallowed a sob. "It breaks my heart that the baby phase of my life is over."

He lifted her chin with a finger. "If I could make things different, I would."

She nodded. "And I appreciate that."

When her tears were spent, Mark pointed at the box. In an obvious attempt to change to a more cheerful subject, he asked, "What's all this?"

Kate pulled her thoughts away from the baby she couldn't have and said, "What I've got to work with to create an award-winning theme for our front door."

Mark raised an eyebrow. "This is it?"

She shrugged. "Pretty much."

"I don't think a magician could create an award-winning door from this stuff," he pointed out gently. "Why don't you just forget about decorating the door?"

Kate ran her fingers through her hair in frustration. "If we don't decorate our door, people might think Christmas doesn't mean *anything* to us."

Mark frowned. "I guess we do need to make an effort, but if you'll wait until Saturday, I'll help you."

She gave him a tremulous smile. Between his new job and his responsibilities as bishop of their ward, Mark had plenty of more serious concerns. "You've got enough to worry about. I'll come up with something."

"You'll come up with something great," he said with an encouraging smile.

"I doubt it," she contradicted him. Then she wrapped her arms around his neck. "But thanks for the vote of confidence."

Instead of speaking, he pressed his lips gently to hers. A few minutes later they were interrupted by the arrival of Miss Eugenia.

"Well, excuse me if I'm intruding," she said as she walked into the room. "I knocked on the back

BETSY BRANNON GREEN

door, but I guess you were too busy kissing to hear me." Lady barked in corroboration from the basket hooked over Miss Eugenia's arm.

Mark stepped away from his wife and greeted their neighbor. "Good morning. Were we expecting you?"

The elderly woman narrowed her eyes at him as she reached up to straighten the ancient pillbox hat perched on her white-gray hair. "I didn't have an appointment if that's what you mean," she replied. "I was on my way to the Haggerty Garden Club's annual Christmas brunch and thought I'd see if Kate wanted to go along—since she doesn't have children in the morning anymore."

"I appreciate the invitation," Kate said, wiping away the tears that still clung to her cheeks. "But I'm about to decorate my front door."

"And not a moment too soon," Miss Eugenia said. After scanning the box of discards, Miss Eugenia returned her gaze to Kate. "Unless your theme is 'Christmas in the Junkyard,' that stuff won't help you."

Kate tried to laugh, but it came out more like a moan, and Miss Eugenia studied her shrewdly. "You've been crying," she said. "You miss Emily and Charles."

Kate didn't correct Miss Eugenia since this *was* true, even if it wasn't the reason for her tears. Emily was now attending a half-day preschool class and a neighbor with a son the same age as Charles had talked Kate into letting him come over and play while Emily was in school. This left Kate alone each morning, and she did miss her children desperately.

"I know it's hard," Miss Eugenia commiserated. "But little Charles needs to be around children his own age, and Miss Bonnie's Kindergarten is a Haggerty tradition."

Kate shrugged. "Emily could have waited until next year for real kindergarten."

Miss Eugenia shook her head. "There's much more to learn these days, so children need to start young! And Miss Bonnie has a very comprehensive curriculum. She teaches Spanish words and tap dancing and even baton twirling."

Mark looked at Kate. "You never know when the ability to twirl a baton might come in handy."

Kate laughed, but Miss Eugenia ignored his remark and leaned down to reroll her knee-high hose. "It's all part of a well-rounded Southern education," she said primly. "I suppose you could insist that the little boys play here instead of at the Ragsdales'."

Kate shook her head. "The Ragsdales have chickens and goats and rabbits. I can't compete with that."

The phone rang, and Mark reached for it, but Kate stopped him. "Don't answer it."

"Why not?" he asked in surprise.

"Because it's probably Sister Park from the family history center. She's trying to get me to research my family tree."

"A bad idea, in my opinion," Miss Eugenia said, stroking the wiry hair on Lady's tiny head. "I know enough about my living relatives. The last thing I want to do is dig up dirt on the dead ones."

"My genealogy has already been done back to Adam," Kate replied. Then she gave her neighbor a sly look. "Maybe even further than that."

Miss Eugenia's eyebrows shot up. "You can trace your ancestry *further* than Adam?"

"No one can trace their family back further than Adam," Mark assured her. "Kate is teasing you."

"Hmph," Miss Eugenia said. "I never know with you Mormons. Well, if you won't go with me Kate, I guess I'll be on my way."

Kate followed Miss Eugenia out the front door, and when they stepped onto the porch she said, "Your door looks nice." Miss Eugenia had decorated her door with a profusion of Christmas-colored flowers. Some were attached to the door itself, and some were in pots on the porch. "Are the potted plants legal?" Kate asked. "I thought all the decorations had to be *on* the door."

"Have you seen George Ann's house!?" Miss Eugenia responded. "She's got that huge angel on the door itself and a herd of plastic shepherds kneeling all the way down her front sidewalk. As if that were not enough, there's the spotlight she borrowed from the community center shining on the angel and a sound system broadcasting the *Hallelujah Chorus* twenty-four hours a day. If she can get by with all of that, I figure a few potted plants won't disqualify me."

"I guess that's true," Kate agreed, turning to her right. "And Miss Polly's door is . . . eye-catching."

Miss Polly had her door covered with shiny red and green hearts. The words "We Love You, Jesus" were printed with silver glitter in the center of each heart.

Miss Eugenia chuckled. "Polly's *heart* sure is in the right place."

"In fact, you could say Miss Polly is *all* heart," Kate agreed.

"It would be heart*less* to continue these awful puns." Miss Eugenia's smile waned as she touched the figurine still clutched in Kate's hand. "The longing for a baby might never go away completely, but it fades with time."

Kate was instantly contrite. Miss Eugenia had never been able to have any children. "Thank you for understanding," she said softly.

Miss Eugenia patted Kate's hand and settled Lady in her basket. Then she descended the steps and headed across the brown grass toward her old Buick. Kate walked back inside and found Mark studying the contents of a file folder.

"I wonder how she does that," Kate said.

"Does what?" Mark closed the file and stuck it into his briefcase.

"Reads my mind." Kate placed Baby Jesus back in the box with the surviving pieces of the nativity set.

Mark laughed. "I don't know, but I wish she'd teach *me* that skill." The phone rang again, and Mark checked the caller ID. "It's Sister Park."

Kate sighed. "I knew it."

"You can't avoid her forever," he pointed out. "If you don't want to work in the family history center, just tell her you're decorating your door for Christmas."

Kate frowned. "Hopeless decorating task or being trapped in the family history center with Sister Park." She enumerated her options. "It's a hard choice."

Mark smiled as he picked up the phone. "Hello." After a brief pause, he winked at Kate. "Yes, Sister Park, she's right here." He extended the phone. "It's for you."

"Thanks a lot," she said with a scowl.

He kissed her cheek. "I'll see you tonight."

She nodded vaguely, then turned her attention to the family history center's director—who never took no for an answer.

CHAPTER THREE

When Mark called home an hour later, Kate was on her way out the door, headed to the family history center in Albany.

"Well, it didn't take Sister Park long to convince you," he said.

"We cut a deal," Kate replied. "Emily needs an angel costume for the Christmas pageant at Miss Bonnie's Kindergarten, and Sister Park offered to make it for me if I'll come to the family history center this morning."

Mark laughed. "Sounds like you got the better end of that deal."

"Time will tell," she muttered.

* * *

When Kate arrived at the family history center, she explained to Sister Park that all her genealogical work was complete. "So my coming here was kind of a waste of time."

Instead of disputing Kate's statement, Sister Park said, "In that case, I have a project for you."

Defeated, Kate sat down in front of a computer terminal.

"Have you ever met Sister Keller?"

Kate considered this for a few seconds. "No, but I've heard Mark mention her. Isn't she a hundred years old and lives in a nursing home?"

Sister Park leaned over Kate's shoulder and entered commands into the computer with practiced ease. "She's ninety-six and has a live-in nurse companion who cares for her at home."

Kate shrugged. She'd been close.

"Sister Keller *thought* she had her genealogy done too," Sister Park was saying. "But recently she found out that no work has been done for her aunt's family. They all died of typhoid fever in 1902."

"The whole family died at once?" Kate asked.

"Mother, father, and four little children," Sister Park confirmed solemnly as she inserted a disc into the computer. "Here is the mother, Faith, listed as a child under her parents."

Kate watched the screen as Sister Park highlighted the name of Faith Keller. With a click of the mouse, blank spaces appeared for Faith's husband and their children. Then Sister Park handed her a piece of paper. "This is a copy of a page from the 1900 Census, listing the Stark family." Kate read the names— Edward, Faith, Joseph, Simon, Lucas, and Sadie.

Sister Park put another piece of paper in her hand. "This is the communal death certificate written by the attending physician in 1902. Each family member is listed by name along with their birthplace and age at the time of death."

"The youngest, Sadie, was only two years old when she died," Kate pointed out.

"Yes, it was a terrible tragedy," Sister Park replied. "After you enter the information, I'll show you how to check to be sure their work hasn't been done by someone else. Then we'll prepare a temple disc."

Kate worked steadily for an hour, and by the time she left to pick up Emily at school, the disc was ready and Sister Park was beaming. "I know Sister Keller will be so pleased. Her health is bad, and she wants this taken care of before she dies."

"It was fun," Kate had to admit.

Sister Park pointed to the Wal-Mart sack that contained a few yards of shimmering white material and a McCall pattern. "When do you need Emily's angel costume?"

"The pageant isn't until next Monday."

"I'll have the costume done by Saturday," Sister Park promised as she walked Kate to the door. "And after the holidays you might consider volunteering in the family history center once a week. There are a lot of people like Sister Keller who could use your help."

"I'll give it some thought," Kate agreed.

* * *

Kate drove back to Haggerty feeling better than she had in weeks. She had a bad moment when Emily announced during lunch that the mother of Mary Beth, her classmate, was having a new baby. This prompted Emily to ask Kate if she could have a baby sister for Christmas, and Kate struggled briefly with tears. But for the most part they had a pleasant afternoon.

When Mark came home that evening, Kate was wearing a Christmas sweater. "Don't you look festive," he said, wrapping his arms around her waist.

"I *feel* sort of festive," she told him. "But the door's still not decorated."

He released her and sat down at the kitchen table. "Super X Drugs is advertising a vinyl Santa door covering for $1.99. All you have to do is tape it on."

"Since a vinyl Santa is *not* what Christmas means to me, we'll consider that an absolute last resort," she said. Then she called the children to come for dinner.

While they ate, Kate told her family about Sister Keller's aunt. "Her family died of typhoid fever in 1902, and no one has ever done the temple work."

"The whole family died together?" Emily inquired doubtfully.

"I guess," Kate answered. "The doctor listed them all on the same death certificate."

"If it was an epidemic, the date on the death certificate was probably the day the doctor finally made it to their house and *found* them all dead," Mark said between bites of chicken casserole.

"Are we all going to get sick?" Charles asked, his eyes round with fear.

"And die on the same day?" Emily added.

"Oh no," Kate assured them. "A long time ago people caught typhoid fever from dirty water, but our water is clean." She glanced over at Mark. "Maybe we should talk about something more cheerful."

"I know something cheerful," Emily volunteered. "Mary Beth's mom is having a baby."

Mark gave Kate a sympathetic look, then said, "That *is* cheerful, Emily."

"But Mama says we can't have a baby for Christmas," she told her father.

Charles nodded in mournful agreement. "Mama said no."

"Heavenly Father is the one who decides about babies," Mark explained as Kate stood and scraped her untouched food into the garbage.

"Can I pray and ask Heavenly Father for a baby sister like Mary Beth's?" Emily asked.

After a moment's hesitation, Mark said, "You can pray about anything, Emily. But remember— sometimes the answer is no." During dessert the phone rang, and Mark checked the caller ID.

"It's Sister Park," he told his wife.

"She probably wants me to come back to the family history center tomorrow, and I just don't have the time."

"Then tell her no," Mark advised.

Kate gave him an incredulous look. "You have

met Sister Park, haven't you? She *never* takes no for an answer."

He laughed. "There's a first time for everything."

Kate wiped her hands on a dish towel and walked toward the phone. "If I don't answer now, she'll just keep calling back." Kate raised the receiver to her ear. "Hello."

"Hi Kate, it's Evelyn Park. Sister Keller asked me to call and express her gratitude for the work you did today."

Kate was ashamed of herself for not wanting to answer the phone. "I'm glad I could help."

"Are you and Bishop Iverson going with the youth to the temple next Tuesday?" Sister Park asked.

"We are," Kate confirmed.

"Sister Keller is very anxious to get the Stark family's temple work done."

Kate paused. What Sister Park proposed would require extra time and energy—making this rare trip to the temple more work than pleasure. But resistance to Sister Park's will was futile, so she agreed.

"Wonderful!" Sister Park replied with enthusiasm. "I'll call and give Sister Keller the good news. And I'll give you the disc on Sunday."

After hanging up the phone, Kate told Mark

about their assignment for the temple trip. "I hope you don't mind my volunteering you."

"I don't," he said, pulling her beside him onto the couch.

"Sister Park wants me to work at the family history center one morning a week after Christmas, and I think I'll say yes."

"You might as well," he said. "She'll keep asking until you do."

Kate snuggled against him. "In the hymn 'Know This, That Every Soul Is Free' there's a line that says, 'God will force no man to heav'n.'"

Mark nodded. "I've always liked that song."

"I don't think Sister Park is fully converted to that principle."

Mark laughed. "I don't mind being forced to heaven—as long as we get there."

CHAPTER FOUR

The next morning Miss Eugenia came over early, holding Lady's basket with one hand and a box of Christmas cards with the other. She put Lady down and said, "Since you're *still* not decorating your door, you can help me address these."

Kate knew Miss Eugenia well enough to be suspicious. "Are you trying to keep me busy so I'll forget about wanting a baby?"

"I'm *trying* to get out of addressing my own Christmas cards," Miss Eugenia retorted. "And if I can distract you from your baby blues at the same time, all the better."

Kate laughed as they settled down at the table to write.

When it was time to pick up the children, Miss Eugenia asked to go along.

"I'm not suicidal or anything," Kate assured her. "You don't have to stay with me every minute."

"I know I don't have to stay with you—the very idea!" Miss Eugenia replied. "Actually, *I* need the children this afternoon."

"Why?" Kate asked.

"I promised to visit the retirement home and thought Emily and Charles could sing a couple of Christmas songs for the old folks."

Kate sensed an ulterior motive. "And you think a visit there will snap me out of my self-pitying mood?"

"What I think is that the old folks will enjoy hearing the children sing," Miss Eugenia insisted as she stood and headed toward the door. "Although snapping you out of this pout you're in would be a nice side benefit."

Kate was still searching for an appropriately scathing reply when they reached the Iversons' minivan. "If you'll run by Whit's office first, we'll drop Lady off there," Miss Eugenia said, climbing into the passenger seat.

Kate drove to the square and parked in front of the law offices of Whit Owens. Then she waited in the van while Miss Eugenia took the little dog inside. "I usually take Lady with me to the retirement home," she told Kate when she returned. "Holding animals is very therapeutic, but today I wanted the children to be the center of attention."

Kate nodded and headed for Miss Bonnie's Kindergarten. Once Emily was belted into the backseat, they drove out to the Ragsdale's mini-farm to pick up Charles. He was feeding baby bunnies and had to be bribed away with the offer of a Happy Meal for lunch before their trip to the retirement home.

Miss Eugenia pulled out her cell phone as they left the rabbit hutches. "I'll call Annabelle and see if she wants to meet us at McDonald's."

Kate took the children to the van and had them buckled in by the time Miss Eugenia joined them. "Is Annabelle coming?" Kate asked.

Miss Eugenia nodded. "She said she'd meet us there as quick as she can, so drive slowly. If we time our arrival just right, Annabelle will pay for lunch."

Kate was appalled. "I can pay for my own lunch!"

Miss Eugenia laughed. "So can I, but I'd rather let Annabelle do it."

Kate didn't rush on the way to McDonald's, but once they got there, she flatly refused to circle the parking lot until Annabelle arrived. However, while they were unloading the children, Annabelle pulled up beside them.

"Are you ready to return my punchbowl?" Annabelle asked her sister.

"I don't have your punchbowl," Miss Eugenia returned impatiently.

Annabelle looked into the van. "Where's your ugly little dog?"

Miss Eugenia gave Annabelle a reproachful look as they walked inside. "Lady's not ugly, and she's with Whit. Annabelle, you go ahead and order for us while we grab a booth by the playground. Kate and I want grilled chicken salads, and the kids will have Happy Meals."

Annabelle nodded and walked toward the counter. Kate leaned down and spoke to Emily. "You and Charles stay right with Miss Eugenia." Then she hurried to catch up with Annabelle.

"I'll order the food *and* pay for it," Kate said a little breathlessly.

Annabelle laughed. "And deny Eugenia the pleasure of thinking she tricked me into buying lunch?"

Kate's eyes widened. "You knew?"

"She's been doing it for years. Let me handle this, and you go help Eugenia with the kids. They're twice as smart and ten times more agile than she is."

With a quick smile over her shoulder, Kate joined her children and Miss Eugenia.

After they were through eating, Miss Eugenia told Annabelle that it was her Christian duty to accompany them to the retirement home.

"I don't know if I want to be in the company of a kleptomaniac," Annabelle replied.

Kate was surprised by this remark. "Who's a kleptomaniac?"

"Eugenia," Annabelle accused. "She stole my punchbowl."

Miss Eugenia rolled her eyes. "I did not."

Anxious to avoid a fight, Kate suggested, "It would be nice if we all went to the retirement home together."

"I'll go," Annabelle agreed. "But I'll be keeping a close watch on my purse while Eugenia's around."

"A close watch," Miss Eugenia muttered. "The very idea."

"Miss Eugenia, will you help me get the children strapped in?" Kate requested.

While Miss Eugenia was coaxing Charles into

his car seat, Annabelle whispered to Kate, "I know you think that Eugenia is forcing me to go to the retirement home against my will, but actually, the receptionist there is my Mary Kay representative, and I'm out of moisturizing cream."

Kate laughed as she climbed in behind the wheel.

* * *

The children's little concert went smoothly, and on the way home Miss Eugenia praised them. "Your singing cheered everyone up. Thank you for coming."

"You're welcome," Charles said politely.

"And it was nice of Miss Annabelle to come too," Emily observed.

"Hmph!" Miss Eugenia replied with obvious disdain. "Annabelle spent the whole time talking to that flighty Fawn Waddell."

"I said Merry Christmas to everyone!" Annabelle defended herself. "And I got a tube of Holly-Berry Red lipstick as a bonus for ordering two bottles of moisturizing cream."

Miss Eugenia shook her head in disgust. "Let's get these children home, Kate. They're late for their naps as it is."

Kate tried unsuccessfully to stifle several yawns on the way home, and finally Miss Eugenia asked if she was ill.

"I just didn't sleep much last night," Kate admitted. "I had a crazy dream about a crying baby girl."

"How do you know the baby was a girl?"

Kate shrugged. "I just know."

Miss Eugenia considered this for a moment, then advised, "You have to face reality, Kate. You can't have another baby."

"Mary Beth's mom is going to have a baby," Emily contributed from the backseat.

Kate expelled a heavy breath. "I sure will be glad when *that* gets to be old news," she muttered as she pulled into the driveway.

* * *

The next morning, Kate sat at the table while Mark ate his breakfast. She tried to think of a subtle way to brooch the subject, but finally she just blurted, "I've been having dreams again."

He looked up. "About Tony?"

A few weeks before, she'd had recurring dreams about her first husband.

"No, this time it's a baby crying." Tears welled up in her eyes. "In my dream I look everywhere, but I can't find her."

Mark reached over and patted her hand. "It's probably just because you want a baby so much, Kate."

"I wonder," she whispered.

Mark's eyes drew together in confusion. "What else could it be?"

She turned her tortured eyes to him and voiced her greatest fear. "What if we agreed too quickly to the hysterectomy after Charles? Maybe the doctors were wrong. We could have waited to see . . ."

"Kate," Mark said firmly. "We followed the advice of your physicians, and it's senseless to torture yourself about that now since there's nothing we can do about it."

"I know it's senseless," she agreed, "but I can't help it." She stood and started clearing away the breakfast dishes.

* * *

Kate continued to dream about a crying baby every night, and by Friday evening she told Mark she couldn't ignore it any longer. "I believe the Lord is trying to send me a message."

"What kind of message?" he asked.

"I think we're supposed to adopt a child."

"That's a very involved process. It might take a while for us to get a baby," he warned her.

"I understand that, but I want to go ahead and start the procedure. If the Lord wants this to happen, it will."

Kate could tell that Mark had his doubts, but he nodded. "Let's pray about it . . ."

"Let's pray hard," she told him. "I've got to start getting some sleep."

* * *

On Saturday morning Sister Park called to say that Emily's costume was finished. Mark suggested that while Kate drove to Albany to pick up the dress, he could take Charles and Emily on a door decoration tour around Haggerty.

"Maybe it will inspire us," he teased.

"I'll agree with one condition." Kate turned to Emily. "Under no circumstances is Daddy allowed inside the Super X Drugstore."

* * *

When Kate arrived at the Parks' immaculate home, Sister Park greeted her at the door. "Here it is," she said, holding up the little angel dress.

"It's beautiful!" Kate exclaimed. "I can't thank you enough, and if there's ever anything I can do for you . . ."

"As a matter of fact," Sister Park interrupted, "there is."

Kate smiled. "I've already decided that I can give you one morning a week in the family history center starting in January."

"That's wonderful," Sister Park replied. "But I was going to ask you to do something else."

Kate was nonplussed. "Oh?"

"I called to check on Sister Keller, and the nurse said she's having a good day—just not eating anything—so I'm going to take her some Christmas cookies."

Kate assimilated this, trying in vain to figure out how it involved her.

"And I told her I'd ask you to come with me."

Now Kate understood *what* Sister Park wanted, but the reason behind the request was still a mystery.

"Why?"

"So she can thank you personally for doing all the work for her aunt's family," Sister Park explained.

Kate frowned. "Sister Park, I get the feeling that you gave me more credit than I deserve for that. You arranged everything." Sister Park laughed. "I may have arranged it, but you're the one who's doing the temple work. And call me Evelyn."

Kate was pleased by the invitation. "Okay, Evelyn."

"So, will you come?"

Kate shrugged. How could she say no? "Sure."

Sister Keller lived in a small house south of town. The nurse, a cheerful woman named Ingrid, answered the door and led them to the bedroom where Sister Keller lay propped up against several pillows.

"Merry Christmas!" Evelyn called out as they entered, and Kate seconded the holiday greeting.

"Did you bring Kate with you?" the shriveled little woman asked.

"I did," Evelyn replied.

Sister Keller held out a claw-like hand. "Come closer, dear, so I can see you."

Kate moved up beside the bed and stood there self-consciously while Sister Keller examined her. "Can't see much because of my cataracts, but Evelyn says you're lovely, and I'll take her word," the old woman finally said.

Kate glanced at Evelyn and then thanked them both.

"I brought you a treat," Evelyn announced, holding up the cookies.

"That was so thoughtful!" Sister Keller took a cookie from the plate and nibbled. "Delicious!" She handed the partially eaten cookie to Ingrid. "I think I'll save the rest for later. Now I want to give you something, Evelyn, since you've been so good to me."

"Oh, that's not necessary," Evelyn assured her.

"I want to," Sister Keller insisted. "Ingrid has been cleaning out for me and since you're such a good cook, I thought you might like my cake pans. Ingrid, will you get them?" The nurse left the room, and Sister Keller turned to Kate. "Do you cook?"

"A little," Kate admitted.

"Then maybe Evelyn will share some of my pans with you. They're old, but they still have a lot of use in them."

Kate started to object, but Evelyn shook her head discreetly, and Kate closed her mouth.

"And speaking of old things," Sister Keller continued, "Kate, do you see a cardboard box over there?"

Kate looked in the direction their hostess was pointing and said, "Yes, ma'am."

"Bring it to me, please."

Kate retrieved the box and deposited it on the bed.

"Ingrid found this when she was cleaning out the back room," Sister Keller explained. "I honestly don't remember ever seeing it before. It must have been with the other things I brought here from my mother's house after she died." The old woman opened the box and removed a cameo brooch.

Evelyn stepped closer. "That's pretty and possibly valuable."

"It's old and may have some value because of that," Sister Keller acknowledged. "But according to my mother, Aunt Faith was very poor, so it's unlikely that any of her jewelry was expensive."

"These things belonged to your Aunt Faith?" Kate asked, instantly interested.

"Yes." Sister Keller extracted a stack of handkerchiefs. "See, these aren't made of fine linen like store-bought hankies. They were cut from old sheets and edged with homemade trim called 'tatting.'"

Kate took one of the yellowed squares of fabric into her hand.

"And this is a baby afghan," Sister Keller said as

she removed a small crocheted blanket. "It's pink so it must have belonged to the little girl, Sadie."

Kate's heart began to pound, and her hand reached out of its own accord to stroke the aged yarn.

"I feel terrible that Aunt Faith has been waiting this long to have her temple work done," Sister Keller went on. "She was my father's oldest sister, and she died before he joined the Church. He did so much genealogy I just *assumed* . . ." Sister Keller fingered an edge of the tattered cardboard. "If we hadn't found this box with the family's death certificate in it, and if I hadn't decided to check my book of remembrance—" She looked up at her guests. "I'd have been so ashamed to see Aunt Faith in the next life!"

"Well," Sister Park said briskly. "You *did* find the box, and Kate will get the temple work done for them next week. So when you finally meet your Aunt Faith, you'll have nothing to apologize for."

"Yes," Sister Keller agreed. "Aunt Faith's sad story will have a happy ending."

Ingrid returned and gave the baking pans to Evelyn.

"They don't make pans like those anymore," Sister Keller told them.

BETSY BRANNON GREEN

"I don't know how to thank you," Evelyn said, her voice thick with emotion. "I'll treasure them."

Sister Keller laughed. "That's thanks enough." Then she turned to Kate, who was examining the baby blanket. "You like that afghan?"

"Yes, of course," Kate said. "It's a complicated pattern, and, well, it seems like your Aunt Faith tried to make even simple things beautiful despite her limited resources."

Sister Keller's eyes grew moist. "My mother once said the same thing. Why don't you take the blanket and use it for your next baby?"

Kate was searching for a response when Evelyn said, "Kate can't have more children."

"Oh." Sister Keller patted Kate's hand. "I'm sorry, dear."

Kate nodded. "Me too." She reached inside the box and lifted one of the handkerchiefs. "But I would like to take this to the temple with me if you don't mind. It will make me feel closer to your aunt."

Sister Keller pushed the box toward Kate. "Take it all and keep it!"

"Oh, no," Kate said quickly. "I can't."

"I don't see why not," Sister Keller responded. "It will be one less thing for the boys ranch folks to pick up when I die."

Kate glanced at Evelyn for direction. "But some of it might be valuable."

"Sister Keller has no living heirs," Evelyn said gently.

"Ingrid has already gotten everything she wants," the old woman told her. "So unless you take the box, the contents will end up in a thrift store."

"I think Faith would be pleased for you to have her things," Evelyn encouraged as Sister Keller pushed the box closer to Kate.

"Take it," Sister Keller said. Then she lowered her voice and added, "Please."

"You're sure?" Kate clarified, and Sister Keller nodded. "If you change your mind, just call me and I'll return it."

Sister Keller smiled. "I won't change my mind."

During the drive back to the Parks' house, Kate hugged the box to her chest. "I still feel a little strange about taking this."

"Sister Keller has few pleasures left in life, and giving her things away is one of them," Evelyn replied. "Enjoy the gift."

Kate pulled out the afghan. "Will it hurt to wash this?"

"Probably not," Sister Park replied. "But you might call a dry cleaner to be sure."

Kate shook her head. "That won't be necessary. I have a neighbor who knows everything. I'll just ask her."

CHAPTER FIVE

On the way back to Haggerty, Kate called Miss Eugenia and explained the delicate laundry situation. "I'm especially concerned about an antique baby afghan."

"My mother had a recipe for a cleaning solution that should work perfectly," Miss Eugenia said. "Although if you're going to hang it on the wall or put it in one of those shadow boxes, it doesn't need to be washed."

"I plan to use it, not display it," Kate told her.

There was a brief pause, then Miss Eugenia said, "Well, I'll be over as soon as I can."

When Kate got home, she brought the box into the kitchen. She had just enough time to remove the blanket and the handkerchiefs before her children came running in the back door, followed closely by Mark.

"Daddy drove us all around town twice and bought us candy!" Emily announced.

Charles held up a Hershey bar. "We got you one."

"But it's kind of melty," Emily added.

Kate smiled. "That was very nice. I'll stick it in the refrigerator and let it harden."

Emily's eyes moved to the table, and she pointed at the box. "What's that?"

"It's a gift from Sister Keller," Kate explained.

"Who is Sister Keller?" Emily asked.

"She's a lady so old she can't come to church," Kate explained. "This stuff belonged to her aunt Faith."

Emily frowned. "Why did she give it to you?"

"Because she's going to die soon," Kate told them.

"Today?" Charles wanted to know.

Kate shook her head. "Hopefully not."

"Are there any toys in there?" Emily inquired, pulling on one aged flap.

"No, just brooches and handkerchiefs." Kate looked at Mark. "And a pink blanket that belonged to a baby named Sadie who died very young."

"That's sad." Emily pointed at the afghan. "What are you going to do with it?"

"I'm not sure yet," Kate replied.

"We could give it to Mary Beth's mom!" Emily suggested. "Since she's having a baby girl."

The subject didn't hurt Kate as much as it had before. "I think we'll keep it," she said, and she felt Mark's gaze on her. "But first we've got to wash it."

"We can use it for Charles!" Emily teased her brother.

"I'm not a baby!" Charles responded adamantly. "Or a girl!"

Kate smiled at her son. "No, we won't use it for Charles." She closed the box lid and handed it to Mark. "This needs to be put up somewhere safe— like a shelf in the laundry room."

While Mark put the box away, Kate transferred the handkerchiefs and blanket to the counter to await Miss Eugenia's arrival. Then she made sandwiches for lunch.

"So, tell me about the door decorations," Kate requested as they settled around the table to eat.

"There are lots of nice ones," Emily said with her mouth full. "The Ledbetters have snowmen on their door!"

"*Two* snowmen!" Charles clarified with enthusiasm.

"And a machine that blows real snow on you if

you get too close," Emily added.

"Wow." Kate was impressed. "Cleo really went all out."

"And the Blackwoods have people dressed up to be Mary and Joseph on their porch," Emily said.

Kate gave Mark a questioning look. "How are they managing that?"

"Baptist Church members are taking turns," he explained.

Kate nodded. "As the preacher, Mr. Blackwood should have an endless supply of volunteers."

"Daddy kept trying to go to the Super X," Emily said with a sly smile at her father. "But we wouldn't let him!"

"Yeah, we didn't let him," Charles repeated.

"Thank you!" Kate responded, and everyone laughed.

"What *are* we going to put on our door?" Emily inquired. "It's almost Christmas."

"I know," Kate answered. "And I promise to take care of it soon."

"Knock, knock!" Annabelle called from the back door.

"Come in," Mark invited.

Annabelle walked inside carrying a plate. "I

brought you some fruit cake. Derrick made it, so I'm sure it's good."

Kate took the plate. "Please thank Derrick for us."

"What brings you to Haggerty?" Mark asked.

"Eugenia told me to come over and help wash handkerchiefs."

"That's surprising," Mark said with a frown. "I've never heard Miss Eugenia admit she needed help before."

"She doesn't really need my help," Annabelle told Mark. "She just wants an audience." Annabelle glanced at her watch. "I don't know what's taking her so long. She was supposed to be here five minutes ago."

"Do you want me to go knock on Miss Eugenia's door?" Emily offered.

"That's okay," Kate said. "I'm sure she'll be here soon."

Annabelle looked at the cupboards. "She said we'd need a large mixing bowl."

Kate got out a bowl, and Emily asked, "Are you going to make cookies?"

"No, we're going to watch Miss Eugenia wash handkerchiefs," Annabelle replied.

"Oh," Emily said with obvious disappointment.

"But Miss Annabelle brought some fruitcake," Kate said. "You and Charles can each have a piece."

Emily smiled at Annabelle as Kate cut two wedges of fruitcake. "Can we eat outside?" Emily requested.

Kate nodded. "Yes, but stay on the deck."

Annabelle picked up one of the old handkerchiefs. "Where did you get these?"

"Sister Keller from church," Kate replied. "This stuff belonged to her Aunt Faith who died of typhoid fever in 1902. Sister Keller won't live much longer so she's giving things away. There's more stuff in a box in the laundry room."

"What are you going to do with it?" Annabelle wanted to know.

"After Christmas I thought I'd use the jewelry and a couple of the handkerchiefs to make a shadow box for one of the guest rooms."

"A shrine to Sister Keller's aunt like the one we have for Miss Imogene Riley in the living room?" Mark teased.

"The display in the living room is an effort to show appreciation for the past—it's not a shrine," Kate told him.

Mark leaned down and whispered into Kate's

ear. "Promise me you'll never put my handkerchiefs on the wall."

"You don't even use handkerchiefs," she reminded him.

"Does that mean I'm shrineproof?" Mark asked.

Kate nodded, and he gave her a quick kiss on the cheek just as Miss Eugenia walked in carrying a grocery sack.

"I declare, every time I come inside this house the two of you are kissing," she scolded. "Seems to me like you've been married long enough to be tired of all that."

"Not quite yet," Mark replied.

"I left Lady on the deck to play with the children," Miss Eugenia said as she put her grocery sack on the counter. "Annabelle, before we get started, why don't you go search my house for your punchbowl. I have nothing to hide."

"Punchbowl?" Mark repeated.

"Annabelle's is missing, and she thought Miss Eugenia might have borrowed it," Kate explained as tactfully as possible.

Annabelle laughed. "The mystery is solved. Derrick had taken my punchbowl to an antique dealer trying to find cups to match. Wasn't that sweet of him?"

"Very sweet," Kate agreed. "And I'm glad your punchbowl isn't lost."

"Aren't you forgetting something?" Miss Eugenia asked her sister.

Annabelle looked confused. "What?"

"The apology you owe me," Miss Eugenia prompted.

"I'm sorry," Annabelle said without much conviction. "Now what took you so long to get here? You said we were starting promptly at one."

"That was my intention," Miss Eugenia confirmed. "But when I got back from the grocery store, I saw that several of the flowers from my door decorations were on the porch, so I had to reattach them. I'll bet George Ann pulled them off. You know how competitive she is."

"Oh, I'm sure she didn't try to ruin your door!" Kate didn't particularly like Miss George Ann, but she didn't think the woman was capable of Christmas decoration vandalism. "It was probably just the wind."

Miss Eugenia shrugged. "I wouldn't put it past her, although *her* chances of winning the contest are zero unless they've added a category for Excessive Use of Everything."

"If she wants to win badly enough, she might bribe the judges," Annabelle suggested.

Miss Eugenia gasped. "She might!"

"I'm sure Miss George Ann did *not* bribe the judges either," Kate disagreed. "Even if she was willing to cheat, she's too cheap."

Miss Eugenia nodded in acknowledgment. "That's true."

Kate peered in the grocery bag. "Now what's all this?"

"Ingredients for our cleaning solution," Miss Eugenia said.

"Why can't you just use regular laundry soap?" Mark asked.

Miss Eugenia looked at him in horror. "Because antiques are delicate!"

Mark rubbed a handkerchief. "This feels pretty sturdy to me."

"They probably are sturdy, but they're also old," Kate pointed out. "And we don't want to take any chances."

Miss Eugenia put a handkerchief into the bowl of cleaning solution. "If this one survives, we'll do the rest." She glanced at the afghan Kate was clutching to her chest. "Then the blanket."

Mark moved toward the back door. "I think I'll go play with Lady and the kids."

Miss Eugenia nodded. "A man is no help in a situation like this."

Mark slipped out, and Miss Eugenia let the handkerchief soak for awhile. Then she rinsed it with cold water and spread it out on a dishcloth to dry.

Annabelle squinted at the handkerchief. "It looks the same to me. Yellow."

"We weren't trying to bleach it, just clean it," Miss Eugenia replied. "It's yellow because it's old." She glanced up at Kate. "In fact, some people will make new things and then soak them in weak tea just to get this shade of antique yellow."

"Is she making fun of that wall hanging in your nursery?" Annabelle asked.

"She is," Kate confirmed.

"Give me another handkerchief," Miss Eugenia requested.

They repeated the process until all the handkerchiefs were clean. Then Kate held her breath as the afghan was lowered into the solution. When it didn't disintegrate, she sighed with relief.

"There," Miss Eugenia said as she put the damp blanket on the counter. "That should do nicely."

Annabelle stood and picked up her purse. "Well, now that Eugenia has wasted the better part of my afternoon, I'll go home."

"Like you have anything important to do," Miss Eugenia responded.

Annabelle headed toward the door. "It's a good thing I wasn't expecting gratitude," she told Kate.

Kate laughed. "Thanks again for the fruitcake."

"You're very welcome," Annabelle said.

After Annabelle left, Kate was admiring the pale pink baby blanket when the front doorbell rang. "I wonder who that could be."

Miss Eugenia was gathering her cleaning supplies. "Only one way to find out."

CHAPTER SIX

Kate walked to the front door and found Miss Polly on the porch. Miss Polly perpetually kept a hand-kerchief tucked in the neckline of whatever dress she was wearing to dab the perspiration that invariably formed along her hairline, but today she was dabbing at her eyes instead of her forehead.

"What's the matter, Miss Polly?" Kate asked.

"Oh, Kate, it's just awful," Miss Polly wailed.

Kate was mildly alarmed. "Come on into the kitchen. Miss Eugenia is here, and I'll pour you both a glass of lemonade while you tell us all about it."

"I declare, Polly, what in the world is wrong with you?" Miss Eugenia demanded when they walked into kitchen.

"My Christmas is completely ruined!" Miss Polly

proclaimed as Kate put a glass of lemonade in front of her guest. Miss Polly took a sip then made a face. "I don't know how you Mormons can drink that stuff," she told Kate. "I don't suppose you have any iced tea?"

"No, but I have milk," Kate offered as an alternative.

Miss Polly pushed the glass away. "I'm not really thirsty."

"So, what terrible thing has happened to you?" Miss Eugenia demanded.

"I am in a feud with George Ann!" Miss Polly announced dramatically.

Miss Eugenia leaned forward, her interest in Miss Polly's plight increasing. "What kind of feud?"

"It all started when we were both named to the Christmas Committee at church," Miss Polly explained. "We had a meeting to discuss decorations for the sanctuary, and I recommended that we use poinsettias like always."

Miss Eugenia nodded. "Sounds sensible to me."

Miss Polly's lips trembled. "Well, not to George Ann! She said poinsettias are old-fashioned—not to mention poisonous!"

Miss Eugenia frowned. "What kind of flowers does George Ann want to use?"

Miss Polly sniffled. "She says magnolia blossoms are more stylish. She says that if we want to compete with the big churches in Albany for younger members we have to be progressive. She says that responsible parents won't bring their children to our Christmas services if the sanctuary is filled with toxic plants."

"*Responsible* parents won't let their children eat the decorations regardless of whether you use poinsettias or magnolia blossoms," Miss Eugenia said with conviction.

Miss Polly twisted her handkerchief. "Why didn't I think to say that?"

"I'll talk to George Ann if you'd like," Miss Eugenia offered.

"No, that will just make matters worse," Miss Polly declined with a sigh. "Besides that was only half of the feud."

Miss Eugenia raised her eyebrows. "There's more?"

Miss Polly nodded miserably. "We also disagreed over the Christmas gift for the preacher and his wife."

"What does Miss George Ann want to get them?" Kate asked.

"A chair to put in the vestibule outside the preacher's office," Miss Polly replied. "She said it's a gift future generations can enjoy."

Miss Eugenia frowned. "But the Blackwoods themselves won't get much pleasure out of it."

"Exactly," Miss Polly cried. "I wanted to give them cash so they can purchase whatever they want for their *own* house. But George Ann says cash is tacky."

"She ought to know," Miss Eugenia murmured. "Since she's hording plenty of it." Then her expression became serious. "Let me give this some thought."

"Maybe you could give the Blackwoods a gift certificate," Kate suggested. "Miss George Ann might find that a little less tacky."

Miss Polly nodded. "That's a good idea."

"Very good," Miss Eugenia agreed with an approving smile at Kate. "But you'll have to soften up George Ann first, in order to get her cooperation."

"How will I do that?" Miss Polly wanted to know.

"By agreeing to magnolia blossoms in the sanctuary," Miss Eugenia explained. "I predict that the congregation will miss the poinsettias and demand them for next year. But in the meantime . . ."

"Miss George Ann will think she won on that point," Kate deduced shrewdly.

Miss Eugenia nodded. "So she should be open to compromise. If you suggest the gift certificate *and* a tasteful plaque to be displayed in the vestibule outside the preacher's office, I think she'll go for it."

"What kind of plaque?" Kate asked.

"One with the names of all the committee members on it so George Ann will get public recognition, which is all she really wants anyway," Miss Eugenia said. "And a scripture engraved in the middle—something like . . ." Miss Eugenia closed her eyes and recited the passage from memory. "Ye shall reap the rewards of your faith, and your diligence, and patience, and long-suffering."

A little frown formed between Miss Polly's brows. "What is that scripture reference, Eugenia? It's not familiar to me."

"I think it's from Alma chapter 32," Kate said, trying hard to hide a smile.

"Alma? Who is Alma?" Miss Polly asked in confusion.

"A Book of Mormon prophet," Kate informed her.

Miss Polly pressed a pudgy hand to her ample bosom. "We can't engrave a saying from the Book of Mormon on a Baptist preacher's Christmas plaque!"

Miss Eugenia laughed. "No, I guess that one won't work. How about the last line of 1 Timothy 5:18, 'The labourer is worthy of his reward'?"

Miss Polly jumped to her feet, all smiles. "Perfect! I can hardly wait to tell George Ann." She started toward the door then paused. "You are all coming for Sunday dinner tomorrow, aren't you? I'm baking a turkey."

"Sounds delicious," Kate said.

"Don't cook it too long or it will be dry," Miss Eugenia advised.

Miss Polly tucked her handkerchief back into the neckline of her floral-print dress. "I may not know how to handle George Ann, but I *can* cook!"

After Miss Polly left, Miss Eugenia picked up her grocery sack. "I guess I'll head home so you can spend the afternoon working on your door decorations."

Kate couldn't think about anything except the baby blanket. "I might wait on that. After all, I don't want to rush into anything."

"Rush! I declare, Kate, Christmas Eve is only a few days away."

Kate nodded. "I know. I'll do it tomorrow."

"By the time you get home from church and eat at Polly's you'll be too tired to decorate your door."

Kate shrugged. "Monday then."

Miss Eugenia shook her head. "Monday you've got to do your visiting teaching, and Emily's pageant is that night. And Tuesday you're going to the temple."

Kate raised her eyebrows. "It sounds like you've appointed yourself to be my social secretary."

"I declare, you need one," Miss Eugenia returned.

Kate laughed. "I won't argue with you about that. And thanks for helping me wash Sister Keller's things. I'm so excited about them, especially the baby blanket."

Miss Eugenia cocked her head to one side. "I can tell that you are, but the question is—why?"

Kate stepped closer and lowered her voice. "Don't tell anyone, but Mark and I are thinking of adopting a baby girl."

Miss Eugenia studied her for a few seconds and then muttered, "Seems like you'd learn to be satisfied with what you have." Before Kate could respond, her neighbor was walking out the back door.

Kate picked up the damp blanket and pressed it to her cheek. Was she being greedy to attempt adoption when she already had two children? Was she investing too much time and energy in a hopeless cause? With a sigh she folded the little afghan and returned it to the box with Faith Keller Stark's discarded jewelry. Then she went outside to play with her family.

That night when Kate and Mark were tucking Charles in, Kate said, "I was thinking that Santa Claus might bring you a racecar bed like Mason's. Would you like that?"

He nodded. "Could it be blue instead of red?"

Kate glanced back at Mark. "What do you think, Daddy?"

"I guess it will depend on how good you've been this year," Mark replied.

"I've been *real* good," Charles assured them.

"Then I'd say a blue racecar bed is in the bag." Mark kissed him and turned out the lights. When they got back to their own room, Mark asked Kate, "Are you sure you want to dismantle the crib? If there's a chance we're going to try to adopt a baby . . ."

Kate removed a nightgown from her drawer. "If things work out with the adoption, we can reassemble the crib. It's unreasonable for me to expect Charles to remain a baby until I have someone to replace him."

"That's very sensible," he praised her gently.

Kate gave him a brave smile. "And speaking of sensible, today when Miss Eugenia was trying to think of a scripture passage for Miss Polly to have engraved on a plaque for the Baptist preacher and his wife, she came up with a verse from Alma."

Mark laughed. "Miss Eugenia is unquestionably the most *Mormon* Methodist I've ever met."

CHAPTER SEVEN

On Sunday morning Mark had to be at church early, so it was still dark outside when he walked into the kitchen.

"You have two choices," Kate told him from her position in front of the cereal cupboard. "Honey Nut Cheerios or Raisin Bran."

Mark gave her a quick kiss on the cheek as he sat down at the table. "I think I'll take the Cheerios. How did you sleep?"

She put the cereal box in front of him. "Fine, except when the baby was crying."

Mark gave her a sympathetic look. "So the sensible approach didn't make the crying stop?"

Kate got the milk out of the refrigerator. "Not yet anyway."

* * *

Miss Eugenia rode with Kate and the children to church in Albany, as had been her custom for years. After the meetings Kate met Miss Eugenia by the Primary door, where they collected Charles and Emily.

"I made you a picture, Mama," Charles said.

"We all drew pictures of the stable where Jesus was born," the nursery leader explained helpfully.

Kate glanced at the piece of blue construction paper covered with crayon marks. "It's beautiful."

Miss Eugenia took the picture as they walked to the van. After a careful study of the scribble, she pronounced, "If this doesn't look *exactly* like the city of Bethlehem!"

"I made a manger," Emily announced, anxious to get her share of adult attention.

"And you did a wonderful job," Miss Eugenia said. "I'm sure a child twice your age couldn't do half as well."

When they got back to Haggerty, Kate intended to change the children's clothes, but Miss Eugenia vetoed that idea. "I want Miss Polly to see them in their Christmas finery. We can tie napkins around their necks to protect their clothing."

Knowing that arguing was futile, Kate nodded and led the way across the lawn to Miss Polly's.

"Don't these children look precious in their new Christmas outfits?" Miss Eugenia demanded when their hostess answered her heart-covered front door wearing a holly-print apron and a big smile.

"You *all* look like fashion plates," Miss Polly complimented.

Kate laughed at the gross exaggeration. "I've been wearing this same red dress every Christmas for the past five years."

Miss Polly waved this aside. "Five years is nothing. Eugenia has been wearing that dress every Christmas for decades!"

Miss Eugenia smoothed the thick polyester fabric of her poinsettia-print dress. "I always say it pays in the long run to buy quality."

Kate disguised a laugh with a cough as Miss Polly ushered them inside.

"Everything's almost ready. Is Mark coming?" Miss Polly asked over her shoulder as she pulled a perfect turkey from the oven.

Kate nodded. "He had a couple of interviews but said he'd get here as quickly as he could."

"Oh, Eugenia," Miss Polly said. "Whit called

just before you got here. His daughter is visiting from Raleigh so he won't be joining us today."

Kate could tell that Miss Eugenia was disappointed, but she didn't comment.

By the time they swathed the children in cloth napkins to protect their clothes, Mark had arrived and dinner was on the table.

"So, how did George Ann like the idea of the plaque?" Miss Eugenia asked as she selected two flaky crescent rolls.

"She loved it!" Miss Polly reported. "Especially when she found out that *her* name would be etched in gold for future generations to see."

"See what?" Annabelle asked as she and her husband, Derrick, joined them.

"George Ann's name on a plaque in the vestibule outside the preacher's office at the Baptist church," Kate explained succinctly.

"Which nobody but George Ann wants to see," Miss Eugenia added. Then she turned to Derrick. "Did you bring some of your broccoli and cranberry salad?"

Derrick removed the lid off a Tupperware bowl with a flourish. "Just for you."

"I'll be glad to put some on your plate," Mark offered.

"Pass the whole bowl down here," Miss Eugenia instructed. "After all, he did make it just for me."

Winston Jones, the local police chief, stopped by during dessert.

"I'm so glad you made it!" Miss Polly told him. "There's a sinful assortment of delicious cakes and pies on the buffet, so help yourself."

"Don't mind if I do," Winston said as he removed his hat.

"And I'd like all of you to be my guests at the annual Christmas Cantata at the Baptist church tonight," Miss Polly invited.

Kate smiled. "That's very generous of you. After Charles snored through last year's cantata, I didn't expect to get a return invitation."

"Little Charles can snore more melodiously than some of the vocal performers," Miss Eugenia commented.

Miss Polly was quick to come to the defense of her church members. "If you feel that way, Eugenia, you are welcome to stay home this year." Miss Polly turned to address the others. "But the rest of you are *definitely* invited."

"Then we will *definitely* be there," Mark promised. "Will you save us seats?"

Miss Polly's cheeks turned a pleased pink. "I'd be delighted."

"We'll come too," Annabelle and Derrick accepted in unison.

Miss Eugenia sighed audibly. "And you know I was just teasing, Polly. I'll be there like I am every year."

"I'd come, Miss Polly," Winston said around a mouthful of cherry pie, "but I'm on duty tonight."

Miss Polly reached over and squeezed Winston's arm. "I understand completely. It's a big responsibility keeping Haggerty safe."

"Hmph!" Miss Eugenia said derisively, and Kate stood up, hoping to prevent more harsh words.

"Dinner was wonderful," Kate told Miss Polly. "But if we're going to keep Charles from making a spectacle out of himself at *this* year's cantata, we'd better get him home for a nap."

Mark stood and helped collect the children. "Yes, I think a nap would do us all some good."

* * *

Once they had the children in bed, Kate and Mark collapsed on the den couch. "What are we going to do with these few minutes of peace?" he asked.

"I should try to come up with a theme for our front door," Kate murmured. "Or I could look through that box of stuff Sister Keller gave me."

"Since you haven't been sleeping well, why don't you take a little nap?" Mark suggested. "And I'll write letters." He stood and spread a Christmas throw over her.

"I feel so guilty," Kate began, but then her eyes closed, and she fell into a deep sleep. She woke up an hour later with her hands pressed to her ears.

"Kate!" Mark's voice called to her through the fog of fatigue. "Kate!"

She opened her eyes and saw her husband's worried face hovering over her. "She won't stop crying!" Kate told him desperately.

"Was it a nightmare?" he asked.

"No, just the same dream about the baby. I can hear her—but I can't *find* her." She looked up at him, miserable. "No matter how hard I try."

He sat down on the couch and pulled her into his arms. "It was just a dream."

She pressed her face against the soft skin of his neck. "I have to find that baby."

* * *

That evening Charles managed to stay awake *and* quiet throughout the Christmas Cantata, so Kate felt doubly blessed as they walked back to Miss Polly's house for one last piece of pie before bedtime.

While they ate, Miss Eugenia solicited help in assembling the gift baskets for the retirement home.

"I've got to make cookies for my visiting teaching route, but maybe I could find a few extra minutes," Kate began.

"If *you* find a few extra minutes, decorate your door," Miss Eugenia instructed her. Then she turned to their hostess. "How about you, Polly?"

"I would help, Eugenia," Miss Polly said. "But I've got to finish the stockings for the children's ward at the Phoebe Putney Memorial Hospital. In fact, I was hoping you could lend *me* a hand."

They both turned to Annabelle. "Don't look at me," Annabelle cried, holding her hand up to ward them off. "Derrick and I are scheduled to work at the soup kitchen all week."

Mark sighed. "I've taken a few days off, so I'm free tomorrow. I was planning to sit in front of the fire sipping hot chocolate and humming Christmas carols, but . . ."

Miss Eugenia interrupted. "You can hum carols while you assemble baskets and stockings."

"Why don't you help Eugenia in the morning," Miss Polly suggested to Mark. "Then you can come over and stuff the stockings tomorrow afternoon."

"Sounds fine to me," Mark agreed.

"Don't forget about the pageant tomorrow night!" Kate reminded them all. "Seven o'clock at Miss Bonnie's Kindergarten."

"I'm going to be an angel," Emily proclaimed proudly.

Miss Eugenia smiled at the little girl. "You always are."

* * *

On Monday morning when Kate picked Emily up at school, Miss Bonnie herself was standing at the curb.

"We have a crisis!" the preschool's director informed Kate.

Kate surveyed Emily quickly, and once she was certain that the child was all in one piece, she asked Miss Bonnie, "What happened?"

"Jessica Jones, the little girl assigned to play the role of Mary in our pageant tonight, has the chicken pox!"

Kate mentally did the math and figured that her family would be quarantined by New Year's Day. Then she realized that Miss Bonnie was still talking. "I'm sorry, could you repeat that?"

"I was saying that we need Emily to fill in for Jessica. One angel won't be missed, but without Mary . . ." Miss Bonnie let her voice trail off, the consequences obvious.

"Do you want to be Mary?" Kate asked Emily.

Emily nodded. "She gets to hold Baby Jesus."

Kate turned back to Miss Bonnie. "What about the costume?"

"All the girls are about the same size, so I'm sure Jessica's costume will fit Emily."

Kate shrugged. "Well, I guess it's settled then."

Miss Bonnie looked greatly relieved. "Wonderful! Emily needs to be here at six o'clock in full costume."

Kate waited until she was out of the preschool traffic before she said to Emily, "That's too bad about Jessica being sick."

"Yes," Emily agreed. "And I'm a little sorry that I won't get to wear my angel costume."

Kate was sorry too, especially since Evelyn Park was planning to come to the production.

"But being Mary is good," Emily continued.

Kate smiled. "Being Mary is very good."

When they got home, Kate let the children watch a holiday DVD while she worked on Christmas cookies. Mark returned from Miss Polly's in time to help Kate fix a quick dinner and then give the children even quicker baths. While Mark dressed Charles, Kate assisted Emily. Jessica's Mary dress was a little big and kept slipping off Emily's shoulder.

"Maybe you could use a safety pin," Emily finally suggested.

Kate thought of the brooches in Faith Keller Stark's box. "Wait right here, Emily. I've got something even better."

Kate hurried downstairs and pulled the box down off the shelf in the laundry room. She opened the flaps and saw the baby afghan. Bravely she removed the blanket and rummaged through the box until she found a large amber-colored brooch. "Perfect," Kate whispered to herself as she hurried back upstairs. She didn't realize she still had the baby afghan in her hand until Emily pointed it out.

"Did that belong to the baby who died?"

Kate nodded, unable to speak.

"Did you bring it so I can wrap Baby Jesus in it?" Emily asked.

Kate swallowed hard. "I think that would be really nice." She handed the blanket to Emily then used the brooch to secure the dress. "I can hardly wait for Miss Eugenia to see you."

Emily laughed. "She'll go crazy when she finds out I'm Mary."

Kate laughed too. "Of course she will. Now it's time to leave."

When they arrived at the preschool, Mark took Charles into the assembly hall while Kate walked Emily to her classroom. Miss Eugenia was waiting by the classroom door. "Bonnie told me that you are going to be the star of the show!"

"I'm Mary," Emily confirmed.

Miss Eugenia gave Emily a big hug. "That is such an honor."

Emily nodded. "And I'm using a special blanket for Baby Jesus."

Miss Eugenia studied the little afghan. Then she glanced at Kate before saying, "I see that you are. Take good care of it."

"I will!" Emily promised as she rushed off to join her fellow cast members.

"Do you think it's wise to let a child play with an antique blanket?" Miss Eugenia asked Kate as they walked toward the assembly hall.

"I think Faith Stark would want that blanket put to good use," Kate said. "Now look for Mark and Charles. Hopefully they found decent seats."

Mark and Charles were reserving an entire row near the front. Annabelle and Derrick had already arrived, along with Miss Polly and Evelyn Park. When Kate saw the family history center director, she apologized that the angel costume wasn't being used.

"Circumstances beyond anyone's control," Evelyn said courteously.

Kate leaned closer and whispered. "On a happier note, Baby Jesus will be wrapped in the afghan from Sister Keller's box."

Evelyn smiled. "As soon as I get home, I'll call Sister Keller and tell her."

Emily's performance was flawless, and the entire event a huge success. Annabelle and Derrick insisted on taking everyone out for ice cream afterward, and it was late by the time the Iversons arrived at home.

As Kate helped Emily undress, the little girl said, "I took good care of the blanket."

Kate looked at the afghan, folded on the end of her bed. "You took *very* good care of it. And you were a wonderful Mary."

"Do you think she was sad?" Emily asked thoughtfully.

"Who?"

"The real Mary, since her baby was going to have to die on the cross."

"I'm not sure Mary understood everything that was going to happen in the future. But I think on that special night when Jesus was born she was just glad to have Him."

"Were you glad when you had me and Charles?"

Kate pulled her daughter close. "Those were two of the happiest days of my life."

Charles came running into the room, screeching at the top of his lungs and effectively breaking the poignant mood.

"What's wrong?" Kate demanded.

"Daddy said he heard reindeer on the roof!" Charles yelled.

"Daddy is teasing you," Kate assured him.

"You're such a baby, Charles," Emily said with disdain. "There can't be reindeer on the roof until Christmas Eve."

* * *

Later, after they had gone to bed, Kate whispered, "Mark?"

"Hmm . . ."

"Are you awake?" she asked.

"Hmm . . ."

"I wish I could let *you* look for the baby tonight so I could get some rest."

"Hmm, hmm."

With a sigh Kate turned over onto her side and closed her eyes.

CHAPTER EIGHT

Kate woke up a few hours later after a terribly vivid dream. She forced herself into a sitting position, then wiped the tears from her eyes and shook Mark. When he fixed her with a bleary gaze, she said, "I can't take this anymore. Either there's a baby I'm supposed to find, or I'm going crazy. I want you to start the paperwork for us to adopt a baby *tomorrow*. If that doesn't help, I'm going to have to visit a psychiatrist."

Mark nodded. "Okay—paperwork first thing tomorrow."

Satisfied with his response, Kate swung her legs over the edge of the bed and stood up.

"Where are you going?" he mumbled.

"To make a cup of hot chocolate. I've played

hide and seek with that phantom baby enough for one night."

Kate padded down to the kitchen and heated some water in the microwave. While opening the Swiss Miss packet, she thought of Sister Keller's box. "This is as good a time as any to go through it," she muttered to herself. Placing the mug of hot chocolate on the table, she walked into the laundry room, picked up the box, and returned to the kitchen.

She put the box beside her mug and pulled the flaps open. As she removed each item she studied it. There were five brooches in various stages of disrepair. There where three pairs of earrings—all broken. There was a little book of poetry, a partially unraveled lace collar, and at the very bottom, a small Bible.

Kate put the other things aside and examined the Bible. The leather cover was cracked with age, and the binding was loose. Careful not to let any pages fall out, she turned to the second chapter of Luke and read about the birth of the Savior from the Stark family Bible. When she reached the part where Mary pondered things in her heart Kate stopped. Mary had to sacrifice her Son for the sins of the world. Faith Keller Stark was blessed with four children but didn't live to raise them. Holding that old Bible in her hands, Kate determined to spend less time grieving for what she didn't have. Then she closed her eyes and said a quick prayer of gratitude for all the blessings she'd been given.

Kate was already feeling better when she opened her eyes. She was about to put away the Bible when she saw some writing on the front inside flap. Curious, she studied the words. In faded but elaborate handwriting were the names of the Stark family along with their birthdates. Kate let her finger trace down the page and read each familiar name aloud. "Edward Stark. Faith Keller Stark. Joseph Stark. Simon Stark. Lucas Stark. Sadie Stark." Then her finger trembled as it encountered another name. "Emma Stark." Beside the name were the words, "died at birth, 1901."

Kate dropped the Bible on the table and ran up the stairs, calling Mark's name. He met her at the bedroom door in obvious alarm. "Kate! What's the matter?"

She threw her arms around him, laughing and crying at the same time. "I found the baby, Mark! Her name is Emma."

"Kate . . ." he began.

"It's Faith Keller Stark's baby," she explained. "She was born in 1901, so she wasn't listed on the 1900 census. And she died the same day she was born, before the typhoid epidemic, and that's why she wasn't listed on the communal death certificate."

Mark rubbed his tousled hair, obviously trying to process the information. "So the baby isn't on the disc we're supposed to take to the temple tomorrow." He glanced at his watch. "I mean, today."

Kate strode purposefully into their bedroom and picked up the baby afghan. "I'll bet Faith made this for Emma, not Sadie. Faith was trying to get the message to me—that's why I've been hearing a crying baby."

Mark didn't look completely convinced, but he was wise enough not to argue. "We'll have to fix the disc."

She nodded. "I'm calling Evelyn right now."

"Kate, it's two o'clock in the morning."

"She'll want to know about this," Kate assured him. "Trust me."

Kate dialed the number and apologized to Brother Park for waking him up, then asked to speak to his wife. She explained the situation to Evelyn and arranged a meeting at the family history center so the disc could be corrected. When Kate hung up the phone, she looked over at Mark. "I think that I might be able to sleep undisturbed now."

He yawned. "That's the best news I've heard in days."

Kate smiled into her pillow. Then she slept blissfully for three hours until the alarm went off. As soon as she opened her eyes, the fatigue disappeared, replaced with excitement. Today Faith Keller Stark would have *all* her children sealed to her.

When Miss Eugenia came over to stay with the children, Kate showed her the Bible. "Well, I declare!" Miss Eugenia said.

"Evelyn Park at the family history center says it was very common for folks to record important dates like births and deaths in their Bibles," Kate told her. "That information has been there for years and no one knew!"

Miss Eugenia shook her head. "No, Kate. Until now, no one *listened.*"

Mark walked in carrying two small suitcases that contained the white clothing they would wear while in the temple. "Don't get her crying again!" he said.

"Too late." Kate wiped her eyes with the back of

her hand. "And even though I've solved the mystery of the crying baby, I still wish I could have more children."

Miss Eugenia nodded. "Of course you do. Finding this other woman's daughter won't change that. But you'll learn to live with it, just as I have."

Kate put her arm around Miss Eugenia's shoulders. "You're helping us to raise our children. We couldn't do it without you."

"Truer words were never spoken!" Miss Eugenia agreed. "Where *are* my precious babies?"

"They're still asleep, and if you're wise, you'll try and keep them that way for a couple more hours," Mark advised. "You can call my cell phone if you have a problem."

"We'll be fine," Miss Eugenia assured them as she followed them out onto the front porch. "You two drive carefully."

When Kate and Mark arrived at the family history center, Sister Park was waiting. "I've got things ready," she told them.

Kate handed Evelyn the disc. "Did you call Sister Keller and tell her about Emma?"

Sadness clouded Evelyn's features. "Sister Keller slipped into a coma last night. It won't be long now."

Kate swallowed the lump in her throat and turned to Mark. "We need to hurry."

Kate wanted to think about Sister Keller and the events of the past week during the drive to Atlanta, but the van was full of exuberant teenagers, and it was impossible to concentrate on anything. When they arrived at the temple, Kate said a quick prayer for Sister Keller, then clutching the handkerchief Faith Keller Stark had made from an old sheet, she climbed out of the car and hurried inside.

The handkerchief came in handy a few hours later when she and Mark knelt across the altar in the sealing room, representing Edward and Faith, and heard the words that sealed the Stark family together for eternity.

After the short ceremony, Mark helped Kate to her feet. Pressing the handkerchief to her eyes, she said, "I've turned into a complete crybaby."

Mark gave her a quick hug. "It's been quite a week. You're entitled."

By the time Kate changed clothes and walked to the parking lot, Mark and the other youth leaders already had the teenagers collected and settled into vehicles. On the way home Kate started calling the

Parks' house, but they were almost to Albany before she got an answer.

"Hello," Evelyn said, a little breathlessly, into the phone.

"It's Kate. We got the work done."

"Oh, that's good to hear," Evelyn replied.

"How is Sister Keller?"

After a short hesitation, Evelyn said, "She's gone, Kate. She died about an hour ago."

Kate couldn't stop the tears that leaked from her eyes. "We made it."

"Yes, Kate. I'm sure Sister Keller had a very happy reunion with her aunt."

After Kate ended the call, she looked over at Mark. "Her death wasn't really sad," she told him as tears slipped down her cheeks. "She was old and sick and . . ."

"Much better off where she is now," Mark finished for her.

"I know. But I'm going to miss her." Kate closed her eyes and allowed herself to doze off. She startled awake a few minutes later.

"Please don't tell me you heard another baby crying!" Mark said.

"No!" Kate reassured him. "I just got the perfect

idea for our door decoration!"

Mark frowned. "Don't you think it's too late to participate? The judges will make their rounds at eight o'clock in the morning."

Kate was not discouraged. "That gives us all night to get it done!"

* * *

As soon as they arrived back in Haggerty, Kate rallied her forces. A grumbling Miss Eugenia was assigned to work the phones. "I need you to call people and ask them if we can borrow a picture of their family."

"You mean a portrait or just a snapshot?" Miss Eugenia asked.

"Either as long as it's not too big."

"Is it supposed to be their immediate family or their parents and brothers and sisters?" Miss Eugenia further inquired.

Kate shrugged. "It doesn't matter. The pictures can be recent or old—in fact, a variety would be nice."

Miss Eugenia shook her head. "Sorry I asked."

Kate laughed. "You've been wanting me to

decorate my door."

Miss Eugenia muttered something unintelligible.

"And tell folks if they'll loan us a picture, I'll send Mark to the all-night photo center at the Super X to make a copy so the original won't be damaged!"

Miss Eugenia nodded, then picked up the phone and started making calls while Kate put the children's coats on over their pajamas.

"We really get to go outside in the middle of the night?" Emily asked in amazement.

"Just on the porch," Kate confirmed. "We've got to decorate our door."

"They'll be asleep within the hour," Mark predicted as he deposited Charles on the top step.

Kate didn't argue his point. "Probably, but I want them to feel involved."

"What if nobody brings us any pictures?" Emily asked.

Kate refused to be discouraged. "If that happens, we'll cut some out of magazines. But right now your daddy is going to help me make a neon sign."

Mark's eyes widened. "Neon might be beyond my capabilities."

"Okay, then I'll settle for white Christmas lights

wound around twisted coat hangers."

Mark smiled. "I think I can handle that."

While Emily and Charles ran inside to find wire coat hangers, Miss Polly arrived carrying a picture of herself as a child with her parents.

"You look just like Shirley Temple!" Kate exclaimed.

"I *was* a pretty child," Miss Polly agreed. "But I look terrible right now." She put a hand to the curlers in her hair self-consciously. "I was dressed for bed when Eugenia called to say you needed my help."

Kate gave her neighbor a hug. "And I can always depend on you. Now go home and get your beauty rest. We'll return this picture tomorrow."

Charles fell asleep before Mark's one-hour prediction and was taken up to bed. Kate and Emily supervised as Mark forced the coat hanger wire to form the words *Families Are Forever*. Then Emily held the battery-operated lights in place while Kate secured them with duct tape. Just as they completed this part of the project, Winston Jones pulled up in his squad car.

"Heard you needed family pictures," he called from the open driver's side window. "So I brought you one."

Mark walked down to the curb and took the

picture. "You were really an ugly little kid," he said after a brief examination.

"Mark!" Kate cried in alarm. Then she addressed Winston. "I'm sure you were very cute."

Winston laughed and waved to Kate. "Good night."

"Thanks!" Kate called after him.

Before Kate could scold Mark for teasing Winston, Miss George Ann Simmons arrived with a picture for the door.

"This is a picture of me and my daddy in front of the Haggerty Baptist Church during its construction," Miss George Ann told Kate.

"Yes, I believe I remember you mentioning that your father donated the land for the church to be built on," Kate replied.

"I'm sure you do remember since she mentions it every chance she gets," Miss Eugenia said from just inside the door.

"Well I never," Miss George Ann sputtered as Cleo Ledbetter arrived with her son, Earl Jr., in tow.

"Let me guess," Kate said as she studied the little boy who was dressed in miniature combat fatigues. "You're a soldier."

"Yes, ma'am!" Earl Jr. bellowed, and Kate stepped

back, startled.

Cleo sighed. "I'm not crazy about this stage. He's always marching and saluting and hollers everything he says. My favorite stage was when he wanted to be a doctor. I never had a bit of trouble getting him to wash his hands back then. All I had to do was say he needed to scrub up." Cleo extended an 11x14 portrait of her family. "You sure you want to put this on your door?"

Kate smiled. "I'm sure. We'll make a copy and return the original to you."

"Don't bother," Cleo said. "I've got a hundred of them."

"And more money than sense," Miss George Ann whispered loudly.

Cleo heard but wasn't offended. "I used to have more sense than money, Miss George Ann, and if I have to choose, I'll take being rich." She turned to her son. "Come on, Sergeant Ledbetter. We'd better get you home before your superior officer finds out you're AWOL."

Kate wasn't sure if she should salute Earl Jr. good-bye, so she just waved.

Then Cornelia Blackwood stepped up and commanded her attention. "I've brought you a picture like Miss Eugenia requested."

"And I appreciate your help very much." Kate reached out to take the photograph, but Cornelia held on tight. "You're going to have to let go, or I can't put it on my door."

Cornelia cleared her throat. "Before I give you our picture, I need to make sure that you're not planning to use it for some strange Mormon ceremony."

Kate struggled to keep her face straight as she nodded. "I promise not to use your picture for anything other than my door collage."

Cornelia seemed greatly relieved. "Then you're welcome to it."

"I hear you have an impressive display at your house," Kate remarked.

Cornelia nodded. "We're hoping to win the Most Religious category. But if we don't win anything, it's been a wonderful ministry to the people of Haggerty."

"That's the way to look at it," Kate agreed.

"Well, I'd better get home." Cornelia gave her picture one last anxious look. "Good luck with your door."

"Thanks," Kate said as Mark came up behind

her, holding his car keys.

"Would you like me to give you a ride, Mrs. Blackwood?" he offered.

"No, thank you," Cornelia declined. "I find the night breeze quite refreshing."

"Where are you going?" Kate asked Mark after Cornelia's departure.

"To the Super X to copy pictures," he replied. "Are you sure you don't want me to pick up a vinyl Santa door cover while I'm there? Since it's almost Christmas Eve, they might have them marked down to half price?"

Kate laughed. "No, I'm committed to this decorating scheme."

"Well, you can get me some doughnuts and apple cider," Miss Eugenia called from the doorway. "If I have to stay up all night, at least I can have something to eat!"

Mark considered her request. "I'm not sure what kind of selection they have at the Super X, but I'll get what I can."

While Mark was gone, several other people brought pictures, so when he walked in with refreshments, Kate had to tell him that another trip would be necessary.

Finally, a little after midnight, Kate put the last picture in place. Then she had Miss Eugenia, Mark, and a sleepy Emily stand in the front yard while she turned on the lights.

"It's so pretty!" Emily said in approval.

Miss Eugenia was less enthusiastic. "At least you've got something on your door."

"Come see." Mark motioned for his wife to join them.

Kate hurried down and looked up at their creation. "I love it!" she cried when she saw the familiar faces glowing in the soft light cast by *Families Are Forever*.

"You might win the award for Best Community Involvement," Miss Eugenia allowed grudgingly. "But the sign won't show up as well in the daylight, and for the life of me, I can't see how it explains what Christmas means to you."

"Finding Faith Stark's baby helped me to focus more clearly on important things," Kate explained. "Families are what Christmas and *life* are all about. Heavenly Father sent His Only Begotten Son to earth to set a perfect example and eventually die for us because *we* are His children too. He loves us and wants us to return to Him. *That's* what Christmas means to me."

Miss Eugenia shook her head. "Don't expect the judges to get all that out of a bunch of pictures and some wire wrapped in lights. I could loan you a few sprigs of holly to give it a little more color."

"If we put holly on the door, it might cover up some of the pictures," Kate pointed out.

"You *should* cover up that one of George Ann and her father," Miss Eugenia recommended. "It makes my stomach churn."

Kate laughed, and Mark rubbed his midsection. "Speaking of stomachs," he said. "I think I'll go inside and have some stale doughnuts. How about you, Miss Eugenia?"

"No, thank you," she replied. "I'm going to take some arthritis medicine then lie on a heating pad for the few hours that are left until dawn."

"I can't thank you enough . . ." Kate began, but Miss Eugenia stopped her.

"I'm too tired for gratitude tonight. Save it until tomorrow." She started toward the white house next door.

"You said the judges will be here at eight o'clock in the morning?" Kate asked the retreating figure.

Miss Eugenia stopped and halfway turned back. "Sometime between eight and nine. Why? Are you really hoping to win?"

Kate shook her head. "No, winning was never my goal. But I do have one final touch that I can't add until the last minute."

Miss Eugenia raised an eyebrow. "Now that gives me something to look forward to." She resumed her trek across the lawn. "That is if I can *move* in the morning."

They watched Miss Eugenia disappear through her back door, then Mark asked, "So, what is the final touch?"

Kate looked into his exhausted, bloodshot eyes and was overcome with tenderness toward him. She reached up and put her hands behind his neck, then drew his face down level with hers. "I want it to be a secret, so I can't tell you," she whispered. "But I promise—I've saved the best for last."

* * *

On Wednesday morning Kate got her family up early, and by eight o'clock she had everyone dressed. After examining each of them individually, she smiled. "Like Miss Polly said—fashion plates," she told the children. "And have I ever mentioned that you look wonderful in green?" she asked Mark, fingering his cable-knit sweater.

"No," he responded with a smile. "But I'll wear it more often."

"What are we going to do now?" Emily asked.

"Now we'll go outside and wave to the judges."

"You want the judges to see *us*?" Mark clarified.

She led him out onto the porch where she had four chairs arranged in front of the door. "Yes, because families *are* forever."

Mark pulled her into his arms. "I love you."

"I know," she acknowledged as tears welled in her eyes. "Now kiss me."

As his lips touched hers, a familiar voice spoke from behind them. "I should have known that the big final touch would be the two of you kissing for the whole town to see!" They turned to find Miss Eugenia and Lady standing in the front yard.

"That wasn't the final touch I had in mind," Kate said as she and Mark stepped apart. "But it's not a bad idea."

"I think that's the judges." Miss Eugenia pointed to a caravan of cars that had just turned onto Maple Street. "So, what *is* the final touch?"

Kate had her family sit in the chairs by the

door. "Us."

Miss Eugenia looked confused for a few seconds. Then she smiled. "Even prettier than a picture. Now I'd better go check and make sure George Ann hasn't pulled any more flowers off my door."

* * *

That evening Kate and Mark snuggled in front of the fire sipping hot chocolate and humming Christmas carols. In between songs they discussed the contest results. "I'm glad Miss Eugenia got Best Use of Color," Kate said. "Her door *was* beautiful."

Mark took a sip of hot chocolate. "Miss Polly is very proud of her Most Appealing to Children award."

"And now she has a headstart on Valentine's Day," Kate added.

Mark laughed then asked, "Are you sorry that we didn't win anything?"

Kate reached into her pajama pocket and rubbed the old, yellowed handkerchief she had placed there. "No. That doesn't bother me at all."

"You seem more at peace with things," Mark ventured.

Kate sighed. "Like Miss Eugenia said, finding Faith's baby didn't take away my longing for one, but it did help. And I'm looking forward to working in the family history center."

"There's usually a reason for our trials. Maybe someday we'll understand."

Kate nodded. "I hope so."

Mark leaned closer. "Do you think it's safe for me to kiss you, or is Miss Eugenia lurking just around the corner?"

"You can't ever be sure when she'll appear," Kate answered. "But I say we should chance it!"

"Merry Christmas," he whispered as his lips descended toward hers.

She closed her eyes and murmured, "Yes, it finally is."

* * *

Eugenia Atkins stared up at the cobweb on her bedroom ceiling, steadfastly ignoring her little dog Lady, who was barking furiously. The Iversons were home and she'd won an award for her door decorations. She had every reason to be happy on this Christmas Eve. But instead she was sad and lonely and missing her husband, Charles.

Reaching down, she gave Lady a comforting pat. "I'm okay, girl," she lied.

Lady whimpered and nuzzled Eugenia's age-spotted fingers.

"I know its past time for our evening walk," Eugenia said listlessly. "I'll get up in just a few minutes."

Lady regarded her with a doubtful look, but before Eugenia could say more, the phone rang. She checked the clock and saw that it was almost ten o'clock on Christmas Eve. There was only one person she could think of who would be calling so late—Annabelle. She grabbed the phone, wondering if her sister had misplaced another family heirloom or if one of their few remaining relatives really had died. "Hello!"

"Eugenia," Whit's voice came through the phone line. "I'm sorry to call so late. I hope I didn't wake you."

Eugenia sat up and smoothed her hair back from her damp face. "No. I was just getting ready to take Lady out for a little walk."

"Well, if you can wait a couple of minutes, I'd like to join you."

"I thought your daughter was visiting from out

of town."

"She just left," Whit informed her. "And I've missed you." There was a brief, awkward pause, and then Whit added, "Lady, too, of course."

"Of course," Eugenia repeated, feeling much better already. "We'd love to have you join us for our walk."

"If you haven't eaten, I thought we could make some homemade pizza. I've been working on a recipe, and I think I've perfected it—but you'll be the final judge of that."

Eugenia laughed. "You'd better hope I don't get tired of you experimenting on me with your recipes."

"I do hope that, Eugenia," Whit said with surprising sincerity. "I hope that very much."

Eugenia opened her closet and took out a green pantsuit that she personally thought was the most flattering outfit she owned. "Well, just come on over anytime," she encouraged him. "Lady and I will be waiting."

KATE'S CHRISTMAS COOKIES

1 cup butter
2 cups sugar
2 eggs
1 1/2 tsp cream of tartar
1 tsp salt
1 1/2 tsp baking soda
2 Tbsp milk
1 tsp vanilla
1 tsp butter flavoring
4 1/2–5 cups all purpose flour

Cream butter and sugar. Add eggs, cream of tartar, salt, vanilla, and butter flavoring. Dissolve soda in milk and add to mixture. Mix well. Add flour slowly until very thick. Refrigerate for 2 hours. Roll out using 1/2 cup flour and 1/2 cup powdered sugar. Cut and bake on greased cookie sheet at 300°F for about 8 minutes until very lightly browned.

* * *

ICING FOR CHRISTMAS COOKIES

1/4 cup margarine
4 cups powdered sugar
Milk
Food coloring of choice

Allow margarine to soften. Add sugar and enough milk to reach a proper consistency. Divide icing into separate bowls and then add a different food coloring to each bowl (you might want to keep one bowl of white icing).

ABOUT THE AUTHOR

BETSY BRANNON GREEN currently lives in Bessemer, Alabama, which is a suburb of Birmingham. She has been married to her husband, Butch, for twenty-seven years, and they have eight children. She loves to read—when she can find the time—and watch sporting events—if they involve her children. She is the Primary chorister in the Bessemer Ward, a family history center volunteer, and works in the office of the Birmingham Temple. Although born in Salt Lake City, Betsy has spent most of her life in the

South. Her writing and her life have been strongly influenced by the town of Headland, Alabama. It was the inspiration for Haggerty and is a place where graciousness and hospitality are still the rule rather than the exception. Her first book, *Hearts in Hiding,* was published in 2001, followed by *Never Look Back* (2002), *Until Proven Guilty* (2002), *Don't Close Your Eyes* (2003), *Above Suspicion* (2003), *Foul Play* (2004), *Silenced* (2004), *Copycat* (2005), *Poison* (2005), and *Double Cross* (2006).

Betsy would love to hear from her readers. If you would like to be updated on Betsy's newest releases or correspond with her, please send an e-mail to info@covenant-lds.com, or visit her website at http://betsybrannongreen.net. You may also write to her in care of Covenant Communications, P.O. Box 416, American Fork, UT 84003-0416.